D0408745

Silver PONY Ranch

Sparkling Jewel

by **D. L. Green**

illustrated by **Emily Wallis**

BRANCHES

SCHOLASTIC INC.

Table of Contents

For Tybe Krasno, my awesome gran. – D. G.
For Mum, Dad, and Lewis – E. W.

Text copyright © 2015 by Debra L. Garfinkle
Illustrations copyright © 2015 by Scholastic Inc.

Library of Congress Cataloging-in-Publication Data
Green, D. L. (Debra L.), author.
Sparkling Jewel / by D. L. Green.
pages cm. — (Silver Pony Ranch ; 1)
Summary: Nine-year-old Tori is thrilled to be spending the summer at her grandmother's ranch, even if she has to share a room with her younger sister Miranda, who is eight — there is a beautiful, but very nervous, new pony called Jewel that she would love to ride, but her grandmother feels that this pony is just too much for a child.
ISBN 0-545-79765-9 (pbk. : alk. paper) — ISBN 0-545-79766-7 (hardcover: alk. paper) — ISBN 0-545-79767-5 (ebook) ISBN 0-545-79768-3 (ebook) 1. Ponies — Juvenile fiction. 2. Ranch life — Juvenile fiction. 3. Horsemanship — Juvenile fiction. 4. Sisters — Juvenile fiction. 5. Grandmothers — Juvenile fiction. [1. Ponies — Fiction. 2. Ranch life — Fiction. 3. Horsemanship — Fiction. 4. Sisters — Fiction. 5. Grandmothers — Fiction.] I. Title.
PZ7.G81926Sp 2015
813.6 — dc23 [Fic]
2014041323

ISBN 978-0-545-79766-5 (hardcover) / ISBN 978-0-545-79765-8 (paperback)

10 9 8 7 6 5 4 3 2 1   15 16 17 18 19

Printed in China   38
First edition, September 2015
Illustrated by Emily Wallis
Edited by Katie Carella
Book design by Jessica Meltzer

$\mathcal{W}$e're here!" I shouted. I pointed to the big SILVER PONY RANCH sign on the gate.

Silver Pony Ranch was named after my awesome Grandma Silver. I had visited my grandma before, but only for a few days at a time. Now that I was nine years old, I was going to stay at the ranch all summer long! My sister, Miranda, was only eight. But she was going to spend the summer here, too. We were so lucky!

"I can't wait to meet Gran's new pony!" I said.

"Ponies are fun. But dogs are even better. Lady is my favorite," Miranda said.

Gran's dog, Lady, was great. But I liked ponies more. I liked ponies more than anything. I peered at the large green field behind Gran's gate. The ponies stood far from the road. They almost looked like toys. Soon, I'd see them up close.

Mom parked the car. "It's so nice to be out of the city and in the country. I hope you girls will love staying here as much as I always did," she said.

"I bet I'll love it even more," I said. I rushed out of the car.

"Me, too!" Miranda said. She followed me.

It felt great to get outside. I loved my sister, but I didn't like being stuck in the car with her. She could be really annoying.

Gran hurried toward us and opened the gate. "Howdy, girls!"

"Hi!" I waved to Gran. Then I raced past her. I wanted to see the ponies!

Silver Pony Ranch

"Come back here, Tori! Come kiss your grandmother hello," Mom said.

I didn't want to hurt Gran's feelings. So I stopped running and turned around.

Gran shook her head. "I'm not kissable now. I just chowed on chili with onions. My breath stinks."

I smiled at Gran, plugged my nose, and blew her a kiss.

She pretended to catch it. Then she said, "Head around back to see my ponies."

Finally! I ran as fast as I could, leaving my family behind.

*A*lbert, Fancy, Buttercup, and Blaze stood together in the field. They had lived at the ranch since I was a baby.

Albert was asleep on his feet as usual. His old, gray neck drooped low to the ground.

I stroked Fancy's fuzzy cheek. She was so pretty! Her brown markings looked like teardrops on her white back. Fancy nuzzled my ear. In pony language, that meant she'd missed me.

"I missed you, too," I said.

She moved her head, as if to nod. Or maybe there was a fly on her face.

My family caught up with me. "Tori, you ran faster than a cat chasing a mouse," Gran said.

Miranda hugged Buttercup and said, "You're my favorite pony."

"Her mane is the same gold color as your hair," Mom said.

Miranda nodded. "I want to braid her mane to match my braid."

"There'll be plenty of time for that," Gran said.

"I can't believe we get to spend all summer here!" I exclaimed.

Gran smiled. "Come on. I'll show you my newest animals."

We followed Gran into her house. Her collie, Lady, sat in a big wire pen by the front door. Three puppies crowded around Lady's belly.

"These fine boys are Lady's triplets," Gran said.

Miranda kneeled by the pen. "They're *so* cute! What are their names?"

Gran shrugged. "I call them Red, Brown, and Gray because of their fur colors. But you girls can name them for real once you get to know them."

Miranda grinned. "Cool!"

"Now I'll show you my new pony," Gran said. "She was bossing around the other ponies. So I put her in a stall in the stable."

"Next time Tori bosses me around, can you put *her* in the stable, Gran?" Miranda asked.

"That's fine. I'll take care of the ponies," I said.

"Girls, be nice," Mom warned us.

We all walked to the stable.

Gran went to fetch the new pony from the back stall. She took a halter and lead rope with her. A halter went around a pony's head. With a lead rope clipped to it, a pony could be led around. Gran was gone only a minute, but it seemed like forever. I was dying to see the new pony!

Then Gran said, "All righty. Here she is!" My jaw dropped. Wow! The new pony was amazing!

~ three ~
Crazy about a Crazy Pony

*T*he most beautiful pony ever stood in front of me. Her glossy coat was the color of hot chocolate. Her mane and tail were as dark as midnight. A bright white star shone between her eyes.

"Meet Jewel," Gran said.

What a perfect name! She sparkled just like a jewel.

"The gal across the way sold her to me. She complained that Jewel tore up her grass," Gran said. "Jewel's seven years old—only a little younger than you girls. And she's just as lively."

Jewel whinnied and stomped her hoof. She was lively all right!

"Oh, Jewel has straw on her back," Gran said. She tied Jewel's lead rope to a post and picked up a currycomb.

Currycomb

"Can I comb Jewel?" I asked.

"Okay. But don't stand behind her. She might kick," Gran said. "I'll stay nearby in case there's a problem."

I nodded. "I can handle her."

I took the comb and placed it gently on Jewel's back. She tossed her head and stomped her hooves.

Mom frowned. "Jewel's not exactly tame," she said.

Miranda wrinkled her nose. "She's *really* wild."

"Jewel does her own thing," Gran said.

Yep. This pony and I were meant for each other!

I tried again to comb her. But she stepped forward and backward. I spoke softly to her. But she snorted and whinnied.

"I'll take over," Gran said.

I hung my head and gave Gran the currycomb. Jewel didn't like being combed by Gran, either. But Gran just kept the currycomb on her. And Jewel let Gran comb her out.

"Can I play with the puppies?" Miranda asked.

"And can I ride Jewel?" I asked.

Mom shook her head. "You girls need to go unpack."

"I'll unpack fast," I said. "*Then* can I ride Jewel?"

"That pony looks dangerous, Tori. Why don't you ride Albert?" Mom said.

"Albert is as slow as a slumbering snail," Gran said. "How about Fancy? You enjoyed riding her before. She's tame, but she has some pep."

"Fancy is a good pony. But Jewel is *amazing.* Can I please ride her, Gran?" I asked.

"Sorry, Tori." Gran patted my shoulder. "No can do. Your mom is right. Jewel is too rowdy."

I let out a huge sigh.

Miranda and I brought our suitcases into Gran's house. Her house was smaller than ours, but I didn't care. I loved it.

Mom led us down the hall past Gran's bedroom. Then she stopped in front of her old room. It had sunny yellow walls, two twin beds, and a cute white dresser.

"This will be your room, Tori," Mom said.

I smiled.

"And Miranda," Mom added.

Miranda and I frowned. At home, we each had our own bedroom.

"I'm not sharing a room with *her*," I said.

"Me, neither," Miranda said, crossing her arms.

"You girls will have to learn to share this room. That is, unless one of you would like to stay in a sleeping bag in the living room." Mom raised her eyebrows.

We brought our suitcases into the room.

Mom smiled. "That's what I thought. And, hey, you might even *like* sharing a room."

I really doubted that.

Then she said, "I need to drive home now. Call me any time if you get homesick." She gave us a big hug. "Tori, take care of your little sister. I love you, girls."

I watched Mom leave. My stomach fluttered as I thought about being away from home all summer long. Then I heard a loud *thunk*. Miranda had put a huge pink box on top of the dresser. It was full of hair bows, ribbons, and barrettes. Most of them were pink.

"Don't cover my dresser with all your girly-girl things," I said.

"It's *my* dresser, too," Miranda said. "Don't boss me around."

Just then, Gran walked into our room. "Girls, you're wasting daylight. The sooner you unpack, the sooner you can get back to the animals," she said.

I stuffed my socks, shirts, and pajamas in a drawer. I shoved my hats and shoes under my bed. I piled my books on the floor.

"Don't leave your things all over my floor," Miranda said.

"It's *my* floor, too," I said. "And there's no time for neatness. I have a pony to ride."

five

Ponies Have Feelings, Too

*A*fter we unpacked, Miranda went to play with the puppies and I ran to the stable.

Jewel's beautiful head poked out of the stable window. Gran stood nearby.

"Hi, Gran!" I said. "Can I *please* ride Jewel? Just for a few tiny, itsy-bitsy minutes?" I widened my eyes, trying to look sad.

"Those puppy-dog eyes don't fool me. You can't ride Jewel today," Gran said. "But you can ride Fancy."

"Okay," I told Gran. Then I whispered into Jewel's ear, "We'll ride together soon."

Gran called for Miranda to join us.

Miranda ran over, smiling. "Those puppies are *sooooo* cute!" she said.

Gran helped us tack up our ponies. That meant getting them ready to ride. We had to put a lot of things on them: a saddle pad, saddle, breast collar, bit, bridle, and reins. The saddle pad and saddle made riding more comfy. The breast collar kept the saddle from sliding. And the bit and bridle went around a pony's head. They attached to the reins, which riders held to guide their ponies.

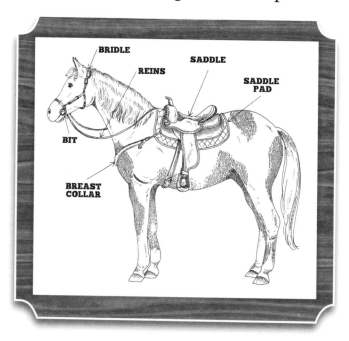

We clipped on our riding helmets. Then Gran climbed on her horse, Blaze. Miranda mounted Buttercup, and I got on Fancy.

I sat high off the ground, like a queen on a mighty throne. I took a big whiff. I loved the smell of the leather saddle, clean pony hair, and fresh air all mixed together.

"Buttercup is such a sweet pony," Miranda said. "I love riding her!"

"You look good on her," Gran said. "Just sit back more."

Miranda shifted her body.

"Much better," Gran said. "And, Tori, you look real fine on Fancy."

"I *feel* real fine on her," I replied. "She's a good pony."

Just then, Jewel neighed. I gazed back at the stable. Jewel still had her head out the window. She stared at me with large, sad eyes. I wished I could ride her.

"Tori, keep your eyes off Jewel and on the pony you're riding," Gran said.

I leaned down and rubbed Fancy's shoulder.

"We'll ride in the arena today, so you girls can get used to riding again," Gran said.

The arena was a large, oval, fenced-in part of the field. It was where Gran taught kids how to ride ponies—and where ponies were taught how to be ridden. We went into the arena.

"Ready?" Gran asked.

"Ready!" we answered at the same time.

"Giddyup," Gran said.

I eased up on the reins. Then I made a kissing sound and squeezed my legs around Fancy's back. That told her to go faster.

We were off! Yee-haw! Even better than riding a pony was riding *fast* on a pony! We trotted around and around the arena. Riding Fancy was so much fun!

But I kept thinking about Jewel's eyes. Maybe she'd tried to look sad for me, just like I'd tried to look sad for Gran. I bet Jewel was thinking, *You shouldn't be riding Fancy. You should be riding me.*

six
Runaway Pony

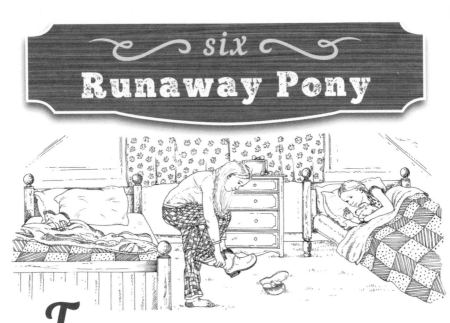

The next morning, I woke up super early and pulled on my boots. I couldn't wait to see Jewel again!

Miranda opened her eyes. "You're going out in your *pajamas*?" she asked. "But you haven't brushed your hair or washed your face or—"

I left the room while my sister was still talking. I tiptoed past Gran's room. She was asleep. I passed Lady and her puppies, and went outside.

The sun was just starting to rise. The cool morning air felt great. I hurried across the field to the stable. Albert was snoring. I giggled as I passed him. Then I reached through the bars of Fancy's stall door and stroked her soft neck.

I finally got to Jewel's stall at the end of the stable. Her head hung down and her eyes were half-closed. She looked lonely. *I could visit her in her stall,* I thought. *Gran* probably *wouldn't mind.* I unlatched Jewel's door and opened it just a little.

Suddenly, Jewel shoved her body past mine. She pushed the door wide open and ran out of her stall.

I rushed after her and yelled, "Stop, Jewel!"

Jewel raced through the stable and out to the field. I chased her, calling, "Jewel! Jewel! Jewel!"

But she kept running. She kicked up clods of grass. And the faster I went, the faster Jewel went. We ran and ran and ran. I could hardly breathe. I could hardly think. But I knew one thing for sure: If Gran found out I'd let Jewel escape, I would be in BIG trouble. And I'd *never* get to ride her.

I had to return this rowdy pony to her stall before Gran woke up!

seven

Cow-Superwoman

I hurried into the house. Miranda was sitting in the puppy pen.

I was out of breath. "Help!" I panted. "Jewel." *Pant.* "Ran." *Pant.* "Out." *Pant.*

"What? All I heard was your very loud breathing," Miranda said.

I took some deep breaths. Then I said, "I accidentally let Jewel out of her stall. Now she's running through the field. Help me get her! Please!"

Miranda shook her head. "No way. I can't catch that crazy pony. Go get Gran."

I frowned. "Do you think she'll be upset?"

"No," Miranda said.

"That's good," I said.

"I think she'll be *more* than upset. She'll be *really angry*," Miranda said.

I sighed. I couldn't let Jewel destroy Gran's field. Maybe Gran could calm her down before she tore up the grass.

I peeked into Gran's bedroom. She was still asleep. "Gran," I whispered.

"Huh?" She sat up.

"Sorry to wake you. But Jewel's running around the field. I can't catch her," I said.

"How'd she get out?" Gran asked as she pulled on her boots.

I didn't answer.

She stared at me. "Did *someone* open Jewel's stall door?"

"Yes." I stared at the floor.

"Well, let's go get her," Gran said.

We hurried out of the house. Miranda ran after us. She held the red puppy in her arms. Gran grabbed a rope. Then she walked through the field toward Jewel.

When Jewel saw Gran, she reared up. Gran tied the rope into a lasso and swung it in the air. It landed around Jewel's neck.

"Wow, Gran! You're such a cowboy!" Miranda exclaimed.

"Cow*girl*," I said.

"Cow-*woman*," Gran said.

"More like cow-*superwoman*," I said.

Gran held onto the rope and walked close to Jewel. She murmured, "You're all right, Jewel," and stroked her neck.

Soon Jewel calmed down.

"Tori, please don't open Jewel's stall again without my say-so," Gran said.

"Sorry," I said.

"You shouldn't have done that," Miranda said.

I glared at her. "*You* should be quiet."

Miranda put down the red puppy and crossed her arms. "I can say what I want," she hissed.

"Please stop arguing, girls. You'll get Jewel riled up again," Gran said. "And, Miranda, pick up that puppy before he gets loose on the field."

"Sorry," Miranda said.

"You shouldn't have done that," I whispered to Miranda.

"*You* should be quiet," Miranda whispered.

I scowled at her. But, really, I was glad I wasn't the only one causing problems.

Miranda leaned down to get the red puppy. But he yapped and ran past her. Then he rushed at Jewel, circling her and barking nonstop. Jewel's nostrils flared and her ears pricked up. She neighed and tried to get away.

"Look at poor Jewel. She's all in a panic over a little puppy who just wants to be her friend," Gran said.

Luckily, Gran kept hold of Jewel's rope.

Unluckily, Gran tripped over the puppy and fell onto her bottom.

Miranda picked up the red puppy. He stopped barking and started licking her neck.

Jewel was still pulling at the rope. So I whispered, "It's okay, Jewel. He's just a little puppy."

Jewel calmed down.

Gran brushed off the dirt from her pajama bottoms. "That little pup sure caused big trouble," she said.

"Trouble! That's it! That's his name!" Miranda cried.

I grinned. "Yes! *Trouble* is the perfect name for him."

"It sure is." Gran laughed. "Well, after this morning's adventure, I could use a big breakfast."

"Me, too. I'm hungry as a horse," I said as I patted Jewel.

Miranda giggled. Then she snuggled with the puppy and said, "I'm doggone hungry."

"How about chocolate-chip pancakes with whipped cream?" Gran asked.

Miranda and I looked at each other. At home, we ate healthy breakfasts, like eggs and oatmeal. But we weren't at home.

"Chocolate-chip pancakes sound super!" I said.

Miranda smiled. "Yeah. Super!"

We returned Jewel to the stable and Trouble to the puppy pen. Then we quickly showered and got dressed. Soon, we were sitting at the kitchen table, eating huge chocolate-chip pancakes with mountains of whipped cream. Delish!

This morning sure had been exciting! And we still had the rest of the day to ride ponies!

nine

Happy Trails Ahead

"Tori, you really gobbled up your pancakes," Gran said.

I grinned. "Well, they were yummy. And I don't like sitting around inside."

"*I* like sitting inside with the puppies," Miranda said.

"*I* like being *outside* with Jewel and the other ponies," I said.

Jewel liked being outside, too. I thought about Jewel's sad eyes watching me ride Fancy. Then I thought about her escape this morning and said, "I bet Jewel gets cranky when she's cooped up in the stable."

"*Hmm*. You may be right. I don't like being cooped up, either," Gran said. "Let's go on a trail ride. I'll ride Jewel and see if that calms her."

"Awesome!" I said. "But *I'll* ride Jewel."

Gran shook her head. "Sorry, Tori."

"I can tame her," I said.

"You can't even tame your wild hair. You'll never be able to ride that wild pony," Miranda said.

I glared at my sister. "I will *too* be able to ride Jewel." But I wasn't sure about that.

"Can Trouble come on the trail ride with us?" Miranda asked.

"All right—if we bring his mama. She'll look after him," Gran said. She patted Lady.

We cleared our plates and hurried to the stable. Trouble and Lady ran next to us. When we got near Jewel's stall, Trouble barked. Jewel neighed, but she didn't try to run away this time. Maybe she was getting used to the puppy.

Gran saddled Jewel, Miranda saddled Buttercup, and I saddled Fancy.

Then we climbed on our ponies. Gran led us on the trail behind her house. She had to pull on Jewel's reins and say *"Whoa"* a lot. But Jewel stayed on the trail. She seemed calmer out of the stable. And Buttercup and Fancy acted as sweet as always.

Lady and Trouble kept up with us, wagging their tails. Trouble ran right next to Jewel. At first, Jewel flinched a little when Trouble yapped and brushed against her legs. But soon she became friendly. She lowered her head near Trouble, as if to say hello.

I loved riding in the country. We waded through a shallow creek. We rode up and down hills and past bright flowers. Squirrels and bunnies darted in front of us. Birds chirped above us.

"This trail ride is perfect," Miranda said.

It was. But it would be even *more* perfect if I were riding Jewel.

After the trail ride, Miranda brought Lady and Trouble back inside. Gran and I stayed outside.

"These ponies look hot. They could use a cool shower—and some shampoo," Gran said. She picked up the hose.

"Can I help?" I asked.

Gran nodded. "Sure thing."

Gran and I washed Fancy and Buttercup first. We rubbed shampoo all over them and hosed them off. It was a lot of work, but fun, too.

Gran looked me up and down. She said, "Tori, you got about as wet as these ponies! I'm guessing you did that on purpose."

I smiled. Gran smiled back. Then she sprayed me with the hose. I giggled.

"Do you think you could wash Jewel?" Gran asked. "I can help if you need a hand."

I wasn't sure I could wash Jewel all by myself. But I told Gran I could. Then I turned on the hose.

Jewel put her mouth near the nozzle. I gave her a long drink. Her big yellow teeth, long tongue, and loud slurping noises were so funny.

I sprayed water on Jewel's back, shampooed her, and rinsed her off. Jewel never tried to pull away. She seemed to love her shower. And I loved making her coat all shiny.

"She's warming up to you," Gran said.

I nodded. "She sure is."

Just then, Miranda ran over. She yelled, "There's big trouble with Trouble!"

Trouble escaped! I can't find him anywhere!" Miranda cried.

"How did he get out of the puppy pen?" Gran asked.

"I braided Lady's fur when she was with her puppies. Then I took her outside. I guess I forgot to close the pen door. And when I came back inside, Trouble was gone," Miranda said.

Her voice was shaky. I could tell she was really upset. "Let's look for him," I said.

"Yes, we'll find him. Come on!" Gran said.

We spent hours searching for Trouble. We walked all over Gran's house and the field and the trail we'd ridden this morning. My legs and feet ached. Even my eyes ached.

As the sun was setting, Gran said, "Come inside, girls. It's getting dark."

"But we have to find Trouble!" Miranda exclaimed.

"We can search in the dark," I said.

Gran shook her head. "No. You could get lost. Then I'd have to search for that puppy *and* you girls."

We went inside.

Gran put a large bowl of mac and cheese on the table. "This should cheer you up. I know it's one of your favorites," she said.

We loved mac and cheese. But tonight, we hardly ate any. We were too worried to eat.

Gran peeked into our room. "Girls, I'm heading to bed. Lights out," she said.

We tried to sleep. But I kept thinking about Trouble. *Where could he have gone? Is he scared? Is Lady upset?*

After a few minutes, Miranda whispered, "Tori, are you awake?"

"Wide awake," I said.

"Me, too. I'm so worried about Trouble. And I wish Mom were here," Miranda said. "At home when I can't sleep, sometimes I braid her hair."

"Do you want to braid *my* hair?" I asked.

Miranda nodded. Then she took a brush and some silver ribbons from the big box on our dresser. She put my hair in one long braid and tied a ribbon at the end of it.

"I'll tie a silver ribbon at the end of *your* braid, too," I told Miranda. And I did.

"Sharing a bedroom is kind of fun," Miranda said.

"It kind of is," I admitted.

"Sorry about putting all my pink stuff everywhere," Miranda said.

I shrugged. "I like pink okay—just not too much of it."

"What if I keep my pink things on my side of the room?" Miranda offered.

"That's a good idea. And I'll try to keep my mess on my side," I said.

"Thanks," Miranda said. Then she asked, "Do you think Trouble is okay?"

I wasn't sure. "Let's go outside and look for him together," I said.

Miranda frowned. "But Gran said it's too dark out."

"Luckily, I have this." I reached under my bed and pulled out a flashlight. "I saw it yesterday when I stuffed my things under my bed. Being messy pays off."

"Being *neat* pays off." Miranda took a flashlight from under her bed. "I saw it yesterday when I swept the floor."

We pulled on our boots.

"Should we tell Gran what we're doing?" Miranda asked.

"No. I don't want to wake her," I said. "We'll be okay. We have flashlights. And we have each other."

"Let's go find Trouble," Miranda said.

Miranda and I tiptoed down the dark hallway. Gran was snoring loudly.

"She sounds like a lion," I joked.

Miranda giggled. "I'm glad I don't have to share a room with *her*."

We kept going. We shined our flashlights under the kitchen table, behind chairs, and all over the house. We didn't see Trouble anywhere.

The longer we searched, the slower Miranda walked, and the more she yawned.

We got to the puppy pen. The brown and gray puppies slept next to Lady.

"Lady looks pretty with her fur braided," I said.

"Yes, but look." Miranda pointed to Lady. "Her eyes are open. She must be worried about Trouble."

"Just like us," I said.

Then we left the house. It was very dark, except for the twinkling stars. "Let's search the field and the stable again," I said.

Miranda let out a big yawn. "I really want to find Trouble. But I'm *so* tired."

"Go on back to bed," I told her.

"But I . . ." Miranda yawned again. "I need to keep searching."

"I'll look for Trouble. You get some sleep," I said.

"Okay. Thanks, Tor." Miranda went inside.

I walked through the field, waving my flashlight. There was no sign of Trouble. It felt scary to be outside in the dark all by myself. I went to the stable. Once I turned on the light, I wasn't so scared. But I was getting tired.

I tiptoed through the stable. Albert and Blaze were asleep. Albert snored almost as loudly as Gran. Fancy slurped water from her bowl. I didn't see Trouble.

It was hard to keep my eyes open. I decided to say good-night to Jewel and then head back to bed. I opened her stall door a bit. I did not want Jewel to escape again, so I squeezed into the stall. Then I latched the door shut behind me. Jewel nuzzled her face against mine.

"Did you miss me? You haven't seen Trouble, have you?" I asked.

If Jewel could talk, I knew she'd say, "I missed you a lot" and "I haven't seen Trouble."

I wanted to show Jewel that I understood her—and that we belonged together at Silver Pony Ranch. I braided Jewel's tail. Then, I untied the silver ribbon from the end of my braid and added it to Jewel's braid.

I gave Jewel a hug, said good-night, and squeezed out of her stall. I shut off the light. Then I left the stable.

As I walked back to the house, I whistled softly for Trouble and shined my flashlight around. It was no use. I didn't see Trouble anywhere. I sure hoped he was okay.

fourteen
Race to the Stable

$\mathcal{E}$arly the next morning, I sat up in bed and gasped.

The noise woke Miranda. "What's wrong?" she asked.

"I just remembered that I forgot to latch Jewel's stall door last night!" I said. I pulled on my boots and rushed out of the room.

"Wait for me!" Miranda yelled.

As I neared Gran's room, she called out, "What's the rush?"

I kept running. Miranda followed me. We hurried out of the house.

"I'll go see if Jewel's still in her stall," Miranda said.

"She's probably racing around outside," I said.

I ran straight to the field, calling, "Jewel! Jewel! Jewel!"

Miranda ran to the stable. Soon she yelled, "Tori! Come quick!"

I rushed over. I heard yapping noises. Miranda stood at the end of the stable, in front of Jewel's stall. The door was wide open. I dashed to Jewel's stall and looked inside.

There was Jewel! She stood calmly by a little red troublemaker. *Trouble!* He yapped at Jewel and jumped on her legs.

Miranda scooped him up and held him close. "Trouble! You silly puppy! Have you been in Jewel's stall this whole time?" she asked.

He licked her cheek.

"I didn't see him here last night. He could have slipped inside after I left though," I said. "I'm just glad he's safe."

Gran rushed in—still wearing her pajamas. "Oh, good! You found Trouble!" she said.

"Yes! Trouble must have come in here to see his friend Jewel." Miranda smiled.

"He barked and jumped on Jewel. But Jewel didn't get rowdy. She acted very gentle," I told Gran. "So . . . can I ride her now?"

"Jewel may be gentle with a puppy, but she might not act that way with *you*," Gran said. "So my answer is still no."

I sighed. Jewel snorted.

"Sorry, Tori—and Jewel," Gran said.

Would I ever, *ever* get to ride that pony?

fifteen
Silver Ribbons

*M*iranda yawned.

"Were you and Miranda up late last night?" Gran asked as we stood in Jewel's stall.

"Sort of," I said.

"Looks like you were." Gran tugged my braid. "Your braids are cute, girls. But next time, how about braiding each other's hair *before* bedtime?"

"Okay, Gran," Miranda and I replied.

"Tori, where's the silver ribbon that was on the end of your braid?" Miranda asked.

"I lent it to a friend." I pointed to Jewel.

Miranda and Gran walked to the back of the stall. They looked at Jewel's pretty tail with the silver ribbon tied around it.

"I chose silver ribbons for Silver Pony Ranch," Miranda said.

"Good idea, Miranda," Gran said. "Can I get a silver ribbon for *my* hair?"

Miranda smiled. "Gran, I'll braid your hair with a silver ribbon, too."

"That would be terrific," Gran said. "Now, Tori, I know you must have snuck out here last night to braid Jewel's tail. But please don't sneak out again. It's not safe."

"Sorry," I said. "We couldn't sleep. So we went looking for Trouble. But Miranda got too tired. And I stayed out—"

"Tori, I understand," Gran cut me off. "And while you shouldn't have snuck out, I *am* impressed that you were able to braid Jewel's tail. It shows that you can handle her. And that Jewel trusts you."

I grinned. Miranda had said if I couldn't tame my hair, I couldn't tame a pony. But I'd just tamed my hair *and* a pony's hair. Now for the pony . . .

"Look." Gran pointed to Jewel. "She's holding her head down. That's a pony's way of saying she'll listen to you. Tori, it looks like it's finally time for you to ride Jewel."

"Hooray!" I squealed. I smiled so wide my mouth hurt.

This was going to be the best day EVER—
for me and for Jewel. "Can I ride her right
now?" I asked.

Gran raised her eyebrows. "Now? In your
pajamas? Before breakfast?"

"Yep," I said.

"I want to ride Buttercup now, too," Miranda added.

"All right. We'll all go for a ride in our pajamas!" Gran said. "But the neighbors will probably think we're nuts."

"They'll think we're having fun," I said.

Gran grinned. "And they'll be right!"

"I'll go put Trouble back in the puppy pen," Miranda said. "And don't forget, we still need to name the other puppies."

"I hope 'Easy' or 'Calm' will suit them," Gran said, laughing.

"Hurry up, Miranda," I said. "I want to ride Jewel right away!"

I saddled up Jewel and put on my riding helmet. Then I led her to the arena.

Gran stood by me as I climbed on Jewel. She was the perfect fit for me. She was strong and beautiful, and totally worth waiting for. She held her head high and her ears forward.

Miranda got on her pony. "Are you nervous, Tori?" she asked.

I shook my head. "Nope. Just excited."

Gran rode up beside me. "Jewel looks as happy as you do," she said.

I made a kissing sound and squeezed my legs around Jewel. She started walking. A minute later, after another kiss and squeeze, she was trotting. Soon, Jewel began to gallop as fast as the wind. Or at least it *felt* as fast as the wind.

I gripped Jewel's reins. She was very lively. But she was tamer now than when I'd first met her. Back then, she wouldn't even let me comb her. Now we were riding together! Ever since I first saw Jewel, I knew we were meant for each other.

"Wow!" Miranda called out. "Jewel runs like a racehorse!"

Jewel was the fastest pony I ever rode. I was flying. It was the best feeling in the world.

"Slow down a bit, Tori. You need more practice before you ride that fast," Gran said.

I didn't want to slow down at all. But I did—because Jewel and I would have all summer long to practice going fast. I wanted to ride Jewel all day today. And all day tomorrow. And the next day. And the next and the next.

Jewel and I were going to have an amazing summer together. We'd had so much fun already. I couldn't wait to see what adventures we'd share next!

D. L. GREEN is a nickname for Debra Lynn Green. Debra is crazy about ponies and puppies. She also loves her family, her dog, Edna, horseback riding, hiking, reading, writing, and ice cream. She does not love lima beans, insects, or cleaning. In fact, she doesn't even *like* those things. Debra lives in California and used to work as a lawyer. She is also the author of the Zeke Meeks series and other books for kids and teens.

EMILY WALLIS lives and works from her little house in the historical town of Lewes, England. Emily loves everything to do with horses—and they're her favorite animals to draw! She has been drawing and painting her whole life. She also loves playing the piano, reading, swimming, cycling, hula-hooping, and exploring! Silver Pony Ranch is her first children's book series.

SiLVER PONY RANCH

Sparkling Jewel

Questions and Activities

*H*ow are Miranda and Tori **similar to** and **different from** each other?

*W*hat are some signs that Jewel is warming up to Tori?

*W*hy does Tori think she and Jewel are meant for each other?

*I*n the beginning of the story, how do Miranda and Tori feel about sharing a bedroom? How do they feel at the end?

*M*iranda likes the puppies best, but Tori prefers the ponies. Write about which one you like best. Explain why, and draw pictures, too.

scholastic.com/branches